My Little Round House

Bolormaa Baasansuren

Adapted by Helen Mixter

Groundwood Books | House of Anansi Press | Toronto Berkeley

IT WAS SO WARM in my first home. My mother's love made it so. But soon it grew too small.

I heard my father's voice for the first time calling, "Jilu, come out, come out. Join us in our ger."

At first I felt cold.

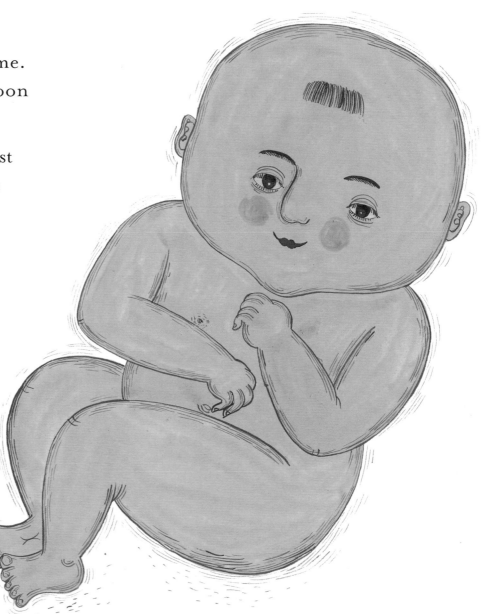

But soon I lay in a soft round bed. My father gave me a little fox that he cut out of felt. It was my first toy.

My mother wrapped me up and held me
in her arms and sang to me. I could
smell the cooking pot, and my round
house felt warm and safe. It was our ger.

When my grandfather came with his
long, long pipe and long, long beard
and gruff voice, I was so scared, I cried.
But then my grandmother picked me up
in her soft arms and bounced me up
and down, and I felt better.

"Jilu, Jilu, my grandson," she hummed.

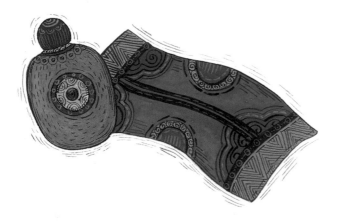

Soon I began to explore. I was tired of staying inside,
so I crept out the door. The grass had turned yellow.

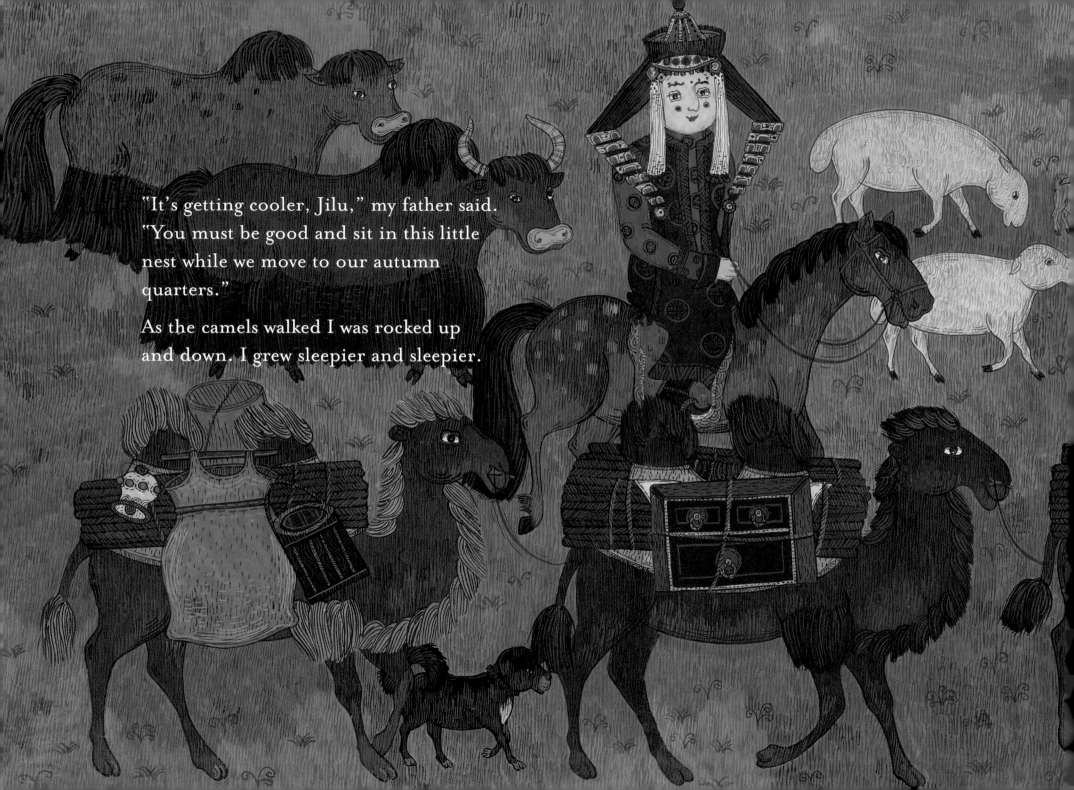

"It's getting cooler, Jilu," my father said. "You must be good and sit in this little nest while we move to our autumn quarters."

As the camels walked I was rocked up and down. I grew sleepier and sleepier.

Before I knew it we were at our autumn camp.
My father and mother had help as they put up
poles for our new ger and then wrapped them in
soft white felt. I could see the sky through the
round hole in the roof.

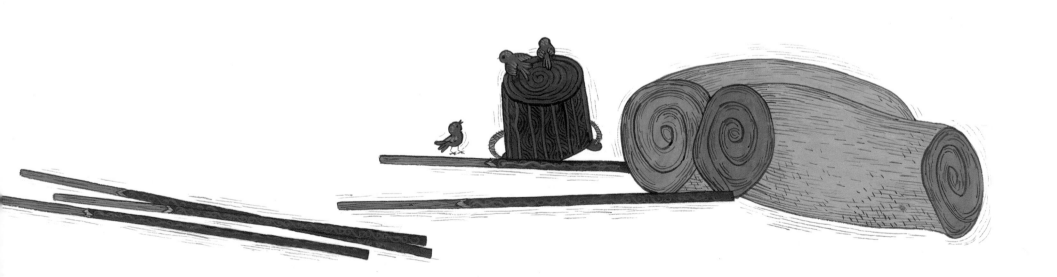

My grandparents came to stay
with us.

"Jilu, be good," my mother said.
"There is so much work to do
getting ready for winter."

I tried to help, too.

One day huge white snowflakes began to fall.
We were off again to our winter campground.
But this time the camels seemed to float along
as their feet padded quietly through the snow.

Once again my parents built a round ger for us.
First came the poles and then felt was wrapped
around and, as always, there was a hole in the roof.
But as soon as they were done, they had to go out
and clean the fences that protected the sheep and
the goats. They were very busy.

The days were so short, it was hard to find time to
play. The nights were so long that we slept a lot.

But one day the ger was filled with people. We greeted them one by one. They had come to celebrate Tsagaan Sar.

My mother said, "This is our most important holiday, Jilu, for we know that spring will soon come again."

The lambs were born. The one with big ears was called Soosoi. The largest was Bumbai and the smallest Mogjookhon. The littlest lambs lived inside our ger with us, and my grandmother gave them milk. I was good at helping her.

Now it was time to move again to our spring quarters. The lambs had grown big enough to run alongside the caravan, and I was big enough to sit on a saddle with my mother.

"Don't move around so much, Jilu," my mother said. "You might fall."

There were flowers and green grass outside our spring ger. We drank fermented milk and ate dumplings in the spring warmth. I didn't need to wear boots anymore.

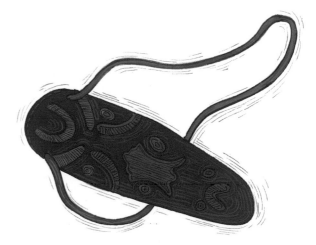

Suddenly it was summer. We moved to our summer
camp where I could play outside in the sun.

Today is my birthday. I am one year old. I run through the grass with the dogs and the lambs and my new friends. The blue sky is like a ger over our heads. This is our home.

Boku No Uchi Wa Gel by Bolormaa Baasansuren.
Copyright © Bolormaa Baasansuren 2006
English text adaptation copyright © 2009 by Helen Mixter
All rights reserved.
Original Japanese edition published by Sekifu-sha.
This English edition published by arrangement with Sekifu-sha,
Fukuoka, care of Tuttle-Mori Agency, Inc., Tokyo.
Published in Canada and the USA in 2009 by Groundwood Books.

Groundwood Books / House of Anansi Press
110 Spadina Avenue, Suite 801, Toronto, Ontario M5V 2K4
or c/o Publishers Group West
1700 Fourth Street, Berkeley, CA 94710

We acknowledge for their financial support of our publishing
program the Government of Canada through the Book Publishing
Industry Development Program (BPIDP).

Library and Archives Canada Cataloguing in Publication
Baasansuren, Bolormaa
My little round house / Bolormaa Baasansuren ; adapted by
Helen Mixter.
ISBN 978-0-88899-934-4
1. Dwellings—Mongolia—Juvenile fiction. I. Mixter, Helen II. Title.
PZ7.B1125My 2009   j823'.92   C2008-905510-1

The illustrations are in gouache on paper.
Printed and bound in China